PITCH HIS TENT
(HOT-BITES NOVELLA)

JORDAN MARIE
JENIKA SNOW

PITCH HIS TENT (Hot-Bites Novella)

By Jenika Snow and Jordan Marie

www.JordanMarieRomance.com

support@jordanmarieromance.com

www.JenikaSnow.com

Jenika_Snow@yahoo.com

Copyright © February 2018 by Jordan Marie and Jenika Snow

First E-book Publication: February 2018

Photographer: Wander Aguiar Photography

Cover model: Andrew Beirnat

Photo provided by: Wander Book Club

Editor: Kasi Alexander

Cover Created by: RBA Designs

ALL RIGHTS RESERVED: The unauthorized reproduction, transmission, or distribution of any part of this copyrighted work is illegal. Criminal copyright infringement is investigated by the FBI and is punishable by up to 5 years in federal prison and a fine of $250,000.

This literary work is fiction. Any name, places, characters and incidents are the product of the author's imagination. Any resemblance to actual persons, living or dead, events or establishments is solely coincidental.

Please respect the author and do not participate in or encourage piracy of copyrighted materials that would violate the author's rights.

Pitch His Tent

JENIKA SNOW
JORDAN MARIE

USA TODAY BESTSELLING AUTHORS

She's my best friend's little sister and completely off limits.
But I'm not going to stop until she's mine.

Beau

I pushed Lexi away years ago.

I've regretted it every moment since, but a man can't live in the past forever.

I decided to go camping to clear my head and plan my future—a future without Lexi.

Imagine my surprise when she's already there.

Lexi knows nothing about camping, that much is clear.

That's okay, I'll use it to my advantage.

I have a second chance and I'm not going to waste it.

First, I'll share my sleeping bag with her and eventually I'll teach her exactly how to…

Pitch My Tent.

Warning: They're back! Jenika Snow and Jordan Marie have teamed up to bring you another hot little number. This time they're taking you out into the wilds. But don't worry, the only thing attacking here is a hero alpha with his eyes set on his woman. A guaranteed safe read that is hot enough to melt your Kindle. It may not teach you how to survive in the wilderness, but if you read closely you might learn the correct way to anchor those tent poles.

Bought and Paid For
Ride My Beard
Planting His Seed
Jingle My Balls
Pitch His Tent

CHAPTER 1

Lexi

"Camping? Like real camping where you're sleeping in a tent in the middle of nowhere, peeing behind trees, and eating beans out of a can? That kind of camping?" Sherry, my best friend since grade school, says in the most disgusted voice she can muster, I'm sure.

Even at twenty-two years old she still gets on my nerves, but makes me laugh at the same time. I stop packing and sit on the edge of the bed. I stare at my hands, knowing that this idea is slightly insane, but something I really need to do for myself. "Believe me, I know how crazy that sounds."

"No, I don't think you do." Sherry gives me a sympathetic look. "Have you even ever been camping before? You do realize you have to have supplies? It's not like you can go to the campsite and they have everything already set up for you." She was smiling, teasing me.

"I'm not a complete moron." I smile back at her. Even though inside I am telling myself there are other things I can do to relieve stress.

"You know if you need to talk I'm here. I'm always here."

I smile back. "I know. I just need to get away for a little while and clear my head."

She nods in understanding. "Yeah, I get that. How long are you going to be gone?"

"Just the week. I borrowed a bunch of camping gear that my brother had stored away, so I'm all set. I just need to get away from the city, from the bullshit of Eddie flaunting his new relationship in my face like I give a shit." I think about my ex. We've been broken up for a month already, yet working with him, and seeing how he nearly fucks the new co-worker right in front of me, as if trying to somehow get back at me for "breaking his heart" grates on my nerves more than I want to admit. Hell, it shouldn't bother me because I'm the one who broke up with him. But I think the stress of work, and the bullshit of Eddie being an asshole has been my tipping point.

"You should just report his ass. Surely him groping his new fling is sexual harassment."

I shrug. "I don't know if it counts as sexual harassment if she's doing the groping too." Sherry makes a disgusted face and I laugh. I get back to packing, and haul the last bag downstairs. I may be only going to be gone for the week, and probably over packed, but I want to make sure I have the comforts of home as I relax.

I toss the last bag in the back of my car. I turn and stare at Sherry. "I'm going to hit the road and get an early start. That way I can set up everything before it gets too dark." I give her a hug and thank her for listening to me bitch. She's the one person I trust implicitly. She's always been there for me, especially in the times I'm feeling like my life is spiraling out of control.

"Oh, I forgot to mention I saw Beau the other day."

Just the mention of my brother's best friend has emotions rising up in me. He's back? Is he on leave? Was he discharged? It's been years since I saw him, years since he and my brother left for a tour with the army. My brother Brooks came home on leave, but I never saw Beau.

I've tried to keep hidden, keep submerged. Beau Sterling is my brother's best friend, his army buddy, and the man I love. He's a guy I grew up around, one who, just looking at him, makes me want to set something on fire. He is arrogant, sure of himself because he knows he's so damn good looking. All through the years I've wanted to slap the smirk off his face, and then pull him in close and kiss him.

It's been a long time since I've spoken to him, yet I'm still consumed with my feelings for him. I can still remember that night all those years ago, right before he left, at the party my parents threw for him and Brooks. I can still remember my lips on his… I shake my head. Nope, not going there.

He's only ever seen me as Brooks' little sister, even when I wanted to be so much more than that. I think that's why I get so pissed thinking about him. Because he never saw me as the woman I am, the woman I grew up to be. He still sees me as that little girl who probably got on his nerves.

But then there's the fact—the secret fact—that even though he pisses me off, I want him. God, I really want him.

I love him.

I've been in love with him since I knew what that word even meant, since I felt my emotions for him rise up and threaten to strangle me.

"I swear," Sherry says, this lustful look in her eyes. "If Beau wasn't such a cocky bastard I might've gone after him." I snort at that. "No, probably not. He's not my type, not in the least." She wrinkles her nose. "But he was wearing a tight black shirt that showed off every muscle." She starts fanning herself. "I love guys in the military, but it's a shame he got injured."

At the mention of that my heart cracks in two slightly.

"And the worst part about it all is he knows how damn good-looking he is."

I laugh, hiding the fact that just thinking about Beau like that gets me all hot and bothered. I feel my face start to heat as I think about him, about how much I hate him ... how much I want him. I say goodbye again quickly and get in my car, not wanting Sherry to see how I am reacting.

Because the last thing I need is for Sherry, or anyone for that matter, to know exactly how much I want Beau Sterling. All that will accomplish is to leave me with a broken heart and nothing to show for it.

CHAPTER 2

Beau

I throw the last of my crap in the back of the truck with a grin. The old truck looks like a rolling wreck, but eventually I'll fix it back. It's a symbol for me. Proof that even battered, with miles on you, you can always start over. When I get this truck restored it will have exactly what I'm giving myself: a new beginning.

Next week I start fresh. After being discharged from the army, I've been at a loss on where to go with my life. Nothing feels right. I miss the military life, but a bum knee that I got as a result of taking shrapnel ended that dream.

My best friend Brooks is still serving and in a lot of ways that makes it worse. Brooks and I have done everything together from grade school up. Where one of us was, the other would be close behind. Brooks' grandfather used to say we were brothers, but I think we were closer than brothers. Hell, I have a brother now I never speak to and, even with Brooks being stationed in Afghanistan, we still talk once a week.

I've been in a rut. It's time I start getting my life back together. That begins with getting my head straight and starting to live again. Since being discharged, that's something I haven't been doing. I had a purpose in the army. Outside there was nothing for me—nothing I could have anyway. There was plenty I wanted... what I've always wanted and denied myself.

Alexandria "Lexi" Clark.

Brooks' younger sister has haunted me since she was five. At first she was annoying. A cute annoyance that Brooks and I put up with, but an annoyance just the same. As she grew up, that slowly changed. She had a quick sense of humor, she was smart, and she made me laugh. There hasn't been much in my life to laugh about, but Lexi always managed it. Still, I never saw her as more than a kid, my best friend's sister. That's it. Then Beau's parents held a going away party for us the night before we were to be shipped overseas. At twenty-four, I wasn't prepared for what was waiting for me across the sea. I sure wasn't prepared for Lexi following me outside that night when I broke away from the party to get a breath of air.

I can still remember it as if it was yesterday. From the yellow and white sundress she wore, to scent of lemons and sugar that clung to her skin.

"Are you scared about going into war, Beau?"

"We're not in war anymore, buttercup. We're just helping that country get on its feet again."

"People die over there all the time."

"People die everywhere."

"You're not scared?" she asked again and I studied her face—really studied it. Her features were etched with concern, her hazel eyes sparkled

with emotions I was afraid to name. I knew Lexi had a crush on me. Brooks knew it too. He made me swear to stay away from her. I laughed it off, telling him she was too young for me and wasn't my type.

I was lying out of my ass.

"Not a bit. I aced all my training. Those soldiers overseas won't know what hit them," I bragged, but inside I was scared. I had never admitted that to anyone. I barely admitted it to myself. Being cocky was how I got through my own issues, how I hid my own fear. I also knew it grated on her nerves, but I didn't want to show her that a part of me was afraid. I was scared to leave the only place I'd ever called home. I was afraid to leave her.

"I'm scared. I don't know what I'd do if something happened to you, Beau."

"You'd barely notice, buttercup." I dismiss her words, even as they make me feel raw inside. No one in my life really cared if I lived or died except for three people. Brooks, his grandfather and Lexi. Of those three, none of them made me ache like Lexi. She made me yearn for more. So much more.

"I'd notice, Beau. I'd be destroyed. I love you," she whispered and then she kissed me.

I pull my mind away from the past. I can't live there and when it comes to Lexi, I want to. Other women may have kissed me in my life. Hers was tame and innocent really. She was only seventeen at the time. I pulled away immediately. I was seven years her senior and she made me want to forget that. That one kiss has been a memory that has lodged deep inside of me over the years. Fitting, since Lexi Clark is the one woman I've never been able to forget.

She's only one more thing to put behind me.

Next week I start my career as an officer of the Montana division of the fish and wildlife agency. It's a new career and a new world before me and it's way past time that I forget the life I used to have and the memory of a kiss from a girl I should have never kissed.

I jump in my truck and turn the key. The engine roars to life and I smile. Things will be different now. I just have to stop living in the past. I'll use this week to clear my head and burn the bridge to my past. I won't look back.

What better place to do that then up on Boulder Ridge, camping and getting back to nature? It's the perfect way to kick off this new chapter and leave the past right where it belongs.

Behind me.

CHAPTER 3

Lexi

"Son of a bitch," I hiss and toss the hammer across the ground, cradling my busted thumb to my chest. It's throbbing because I was a dumbass and hit the digit instead of the spike that would hold my tent down.

I sit on my ass and stare at my half-erected home for the next week. I still have no idea why in the hell I decided to do this. It sounded like a good idea at the time, but now I'm seriously having my doubts.

Exhaling and scooting back so I'm leaning against a thick evergreen, I tilt my head back and stare up at the sky. There's a break between the tree line, which shows a beautiful swatch of blue and white. I hear nothing but the rustling of wind through the leaves, the scurry of some animal off in the distance. I close my eyes and let the wind brush over my skin. The scent of pine and dirt fill my head. This is a very beautiful place, scenic and relaxing. Peaceful.

Now I remember why I needed to do this.

I don't know how long I sit here, but it's the sound of an approaching vehicle that draws my attention. I lean forward and stare at the vehicle I can see in the distance. And as it comes closer I realize it's an older truck, one that looks very familiar. My heart starts beating hard and fast, and just when I think it'll drive past, it actually pulls into the camping spot beside mine.

God.

It can't be who I think it is.

My position makes it hard to see exactly who the driver is, especially with the glare from the sun covering the windshield, causing a reflection of the trees all around.

I wanted peace and isolation, but with my new neighbor I doubt I'll get that now. It's not like I can just up and leave, not unless I want to lose all the money and time I spent in planning this damn retreat.

The driver's side door opens and from my position I can only see a boot emerge. It is big and worn, scuffed, and clearly masculine. And then the guy comes fully out, slams the door shut, and proceeds to stretch. My heart jumps into my throat when I see who it is.

Beau Sterling.

Has hell frozen over right now? I look up at the sky to see if pigs are flying. How in the hell is Beau Sterling parked in the campsite beside me? Is this some kind of cruel, sick joke? He has yet to notice me, or if he does he is clearly ignoring me. Maybe that is for the best.

I can't hide the fact I do have feelings for him. He is strong and smart, and does have a caring side that I've seen a handful of times. He served in the army, got wounded because of it.

I made a fool of myself over him years ago. I was young and naïve and I just want to forget that kiss, forget the way he acted uninterested in me. I don't know how long he's been home, but I hate that he didn't come see me.

It looks like my luck has just run out in keeping my emotions locked down, in pretending I can not be in love with him.

He turns his head and looks right at me. My heart jumps to my throat, my belly clenches tight, and every erogenous zone in my body tightens up. He's big and strong, tall and muscular. The jeans he wears are slightly loose, but they fit him perfectly, showing off his masculinity. The T-shirt he wears is snug, showing the ripples and dips of his muscles, the ridges of his six pack.

His dark hair is short, slightly disheveled. And his eyes, like two pieces of onyx, seem to look right into my very soul, knowing all my secrets. I feel my face heat and wonder if he can see me blushing. My nipples tighten, beading up under my shirt. And I'm wet, God I'm so wet between my thighs my panties are becoming soaked.

How in the hell am I supposed to camp with Beau Sterling right next to me?

CHAPTER 4

Beau

"Fuck!" I growl before I can stop myself. It's a kneejerk reaction and the word springs forth the minute I see Lexi. I watch her flinch at what I said and I instantly regret it. The thing is, when I'm around her I can't seem to stop myself from being an asshole. It's my way to push her away, to pretend she's nothing more to me than Brooks' little sister. I've spent my life pushing her away, it seems. "What are you doing here, Lexi?"

"Charming as ever," she mutters. She gets up off the ground, turning away from me. I bite down a moan when she bends over and her ass stretches against her jeans. Sweet mother of God, there's not a woman alive that can fill out a pair of pants like Lexi.

She turns around, holding a hammer in one hand. I should probably worry she's going to use it on me. Lord knows I've given her more than enough reason to.

"What are you doing here?" I ask again.

"Gee, I don't know, Einstein. Camping?" There's a bite in her voice.

"Camping?"

"That's what I said," she mumbles, walking toward the heap of material lying on the ground that I think is *supposed* to be her tent.

"Lexi."

"What?" she asks, looking over at me.

"You don't camp. Hell, you cringe at the thought of using a public bathroom, let alone going out in the woods." I look around. She's alone. She came out here alone? I don't fucking like that.

"You don't know me anymore, Beau. You never did, really," she says, avoiding my eyes.

She's wrong, of course. If she had any idea just how much I know about her, she would freak out. There was a time in my life where I lived for daily updates about her. Shit, maybe I still do, but I need to stop. Lexi is not mine and she never will be. This week is all about starting fresh and putting the past behind me. Just because the biggest problem with my past has shown up here, nothing has changed. It's just a sign from the cosmic universe that moving on is long past due.

"You still with that Eddie boy?" I ask her. I remember she was with some loser named Edward Winslow the Third. Brooks would bitch about the little asshole daily, and I'd grit my teeth thinking of Lexi with someone other than me. He never fails to remind you of *the third* part either—which is rather stupid, since the dude used to work as a night manager at the local 7/11. Why she ever saddled herself with that waste of space I will never know.

She snorts. "No," she says firmly, trying to ignore me and look at the mess that is her tent. She's staring at the metal pole that loops in the ends of the tent like it's a creature from outer space. I'd laugh if my heart wasn't beating in my chest so hard that it's painful.

"You finally kicked the guy to the curb?" I ask her, alternating between hoping I'm right and praying I'm wrong. It was hard enough to stay away from Lexi before. If she's single... *Fuck.*

"We broke up, if you must know."

"Brooks never mentioned it," I mumble, more to myself than to her.

"Why in the world would he mention it to you? Besides, I'm not sure he knows."

"Why wouldn't your brother know?" I rub the back of my neck, hating that the fact of Lexi being single is getting to me so deeply.

"It may surprise you, Beau, but my brother doesn't really want to hear about my personal life."

"You can tell me all about it," I tell her with a grin, doing my best to not let her know that the news of her being single has shaken me.

"Why? Do you need to take notes?" she asks, sweetly.

"Trust me, honey, notes on your personal life is the last thing I need," I tell her, getting annoyed at the thought of her with anyone. Shit, all I can think about is showing her exactly how much I want her ... as long as Brooks never found out about it. Christ, I can't camp beside Lexi; there's no way I'm going to survive.

She stretches the tent pole she's holding. Too bad it's the wrong part of the tent and she doesn't have the pole set.

I bite back a laugh when once she has it stretched she takes a step back to admire her handiwork and the tent collapses in a sorrowful, sad mess. I look up at the clouds in the sky and sigh. If I don't get a move on with my own tent, we're both going to be sitting out in the rain. If I do get my tent up, Lexi will probably wind up in it with me... which will be a different kind of hell.

CHAPTER 5

Lexi

I stand back and watch as Beau puts together my tent. It's safer this way. I'll end up just screwing something up. He finally came over after me cursing like a sailor for the last hour, trying to put the damn thing together. I had been about to say screw it, that I would sleep in my car, or even head into town and stay at that rinky-dink little motel I passed coming up here, but Beau stepped in and saved the day, something he is good at.

I don't know why I thought camping would be a good idea. And to make matters worse, Beau will be in the site right beside me, like fate is trying to say something. Or maybe it is wishful thinking on my part, like I want things to just fall into place.

"Okay, you're ready to go." He stands and wipes his hands on his jeans, dusting off the dirt. The sun is already starting to set and I feel really bad that he's been working on my stuff instead of getting his own set up. Although he got his tent set up for the evening already, thankfully.

But still, I want to do something to say thank you. "Can I make you some dinner, as a thank you for helping me out?"

He grins, flashing a set of straight white teeth. "I'm not gonna turn down some food, especially if you're making for me."

I feel my cheeks heat and turn away before he sees. For the next ten minutes I set everything up, get the little propane stove ready, grab the can of beans and a can of fruit. I even brought some burgers that I'll grill. It didn't even occur to me to light a fire, but I look over my shoulder and see Beau is already on it. Although dinner won't be a feast, it will be a warm meal and hopefully things can get a little less awkward between us with some conversation.

Another twenty minutes passes and dinner is ready, the fire is roaring, and Beau has two foldout chairs placed around the pit. I walk over to him, a plate in each hand, and give him one. I see he's brought over a cooler, and he pops the lid and wraps his fingers around the necks of two beer bottles. He hands me one and I take it with a grateful smile.

We eat in silence, me just staring at the flames licking over the logs, very aware that Beau is sitting right next to me. Although I'm hot, it has nothing to do with the fire in front of me.

His presence makes me feel very self-aware. I sneak a glance over at him and see that he's already watching me. I feel my face heat even further and look away quickly.

"Tell me what's been going on, Lexi."

Hearing him say my name does all kinds of things to me. He was the first person to ever start calling me Lexi. After that it just kind of caught on with my friends, even Brooks. I shrug, still not looking at him, still not able to make eye contact.

"Nothing really." That's the truth. After he and Brooks left for the military I basically puttered around. I finished school and got my associates degree in business, but I'm not exactly using it.

I look Beau in the eyes and this strong feeling overcomes me. I want to tell him how much I love him, want to tell him that him being away all these years was hard. I want to ask him how long he's been back. I want to ask him why he didn't come see me.

But even though all these questions are running through my mind, I know I'll never ask them. I'm too afraid, too frightened of his reaction, of his response. I've dreamed so many times about telling him, and he reciprocated my feelings, pulled me in close and told me he loved me. Those were the dreams of a silly girl, though, and I told myself that every time.

But what if? What if I was finally honest and the attraction wasn't just one-way?

CHAPTER 6

Beau

I finish up my food, feeling disappointed. I hate that things between us are stilted. I realize it's partly my fault. Lexi is still upset because I rejected her after the kiss all those years ago. It's probably for the best she thinks that way.

"I guess I'll go finish setting up my camp, Lexi. Thanks for dinner."

"You're leaving?" she asks and she sounds surprised. It can't have escaped her notice that we're barely talking to each other.

"Yeah I need to get my camp ready or I'll be sleeping on the ground." I grin. "The weather report predicted some heavy rain coming in late tonight."

"It did?" she asks, and it's clear she had no idea. What kind of person plans a camping trip without checking the weather? I could have laughed. She's too damn cute.

I pinch the bridge of my nose and hold my head down. Does Brooks even know what his sister is up to? How could he allow her to be out here camping all alone, without any protection? He didn't want me to touch her, then the least the asshole could have done was to make sure she didn't do stupid stuff like this. She needs a man to take care of her.

"Yeah. It did. When most people decide to camp, Lexi, they check the weather so they are sure to be prepared." I exhale a breath of frustration and let it go. Lexi is not the kind of girl to like the outdoors. She'll be gone tomorrow and this won't matter.

"Anyway, it's not like you're really talking to me, so I'm going to go," I growl, turning into an instant asshole because she needs a man to take care of her, and I know it can't be me.

"I was talking! Maybe you're just pouting because I'm not falling at your feet like most girls do."

"I didn't realize you'd been watching what other girls do," I respond, looking at her. I'm watching her closely so I can see the minute that the flush enters her face, even when she moves, putting away her trash, trying to avoid my stare.

"I wasn't. Not really. I just know what Brooks tells me."

That answer annoys me instantly. Hell, Brooks hasn't seen me since I was discharged. He's still living the life I thought I would. Deployed overseas and well on his way to being a general. There's a part of me that resents him for that, but he's my best friend. He's not responsible for the shambles my life is in. Brooks may have made it clear his sister was off limits, even if he didn't know I wanted her, and I might be honoring that, but shit, I knew Lexi cared about me. I could see it in her eyes and the way she looked at me. I never wanted to hurt her—even inadvertently. Lexi has always been in my heart.

Which can only mean that Brooks has been spreading lies to drive Lexi further away from me.

"Do you believe everything you're told?"

"Brooks wouldn't lie to me. Besides, it's not like it is any of my business. You made it clear how you felt about me years ago, Beau."

"Just because I told you that I...that we shouldn't..."

"You told me not to kiss you anymore, that I was a kid, even though I wasn't. You told me I wasn't your type. Trust me, Beau, I remember. I got the message back then loud and clear, and I get the message now. Thanks for helping me with my tent. I think I'll turn in."

"Why does everything with you end in a fight?" I growl. "It's good you'll be leaving tomorrow. I came up here to get peace, not more stress."

"I'm not leaving tomorrow. I have this campground rented for the whole week and that's exactly how long I'm staying."

"You? You're planning on staying out in the wild all week? No fucking way."

"What's so hard to believe about that?"

"You forget I know you, buttercup."

"Don't call me that."

"You used to love it when I called you buttercup."

"I don't anymore. I've changed. *You* don't know me anymore, Beau."

"I know you don't like living without modern conveniences. I know your idea of roughing it is spending the night without internet, *not* indoor plumbing."

"Like I said, Beau Sterling, you don't know me anymore," she says, dismissing me without looking back and making her way to her tent.

I don't know what pisses me off more. It could be the fact that she's walking away from me, it could be the fact she asked me to stop calling her my nickname, or it could even be the coolness she's treating me with. I think, however, it has more to do with the fact that she's right. I don't really know Lexi anymore. I've been spending my life pushing her away and avoiding her. I didn't want to. I did it out of respect for Brooks and his wishes, but I still did it.

I've regretted it every day, but more so right now than ever.

"I'll tell you what I do know."

"What's that?" she asks, not bothering to turn around and sounding very bored.

"I know that cheap little pink tent you bought isn't going to stand up to the thunderstorms we're supposed to get. If you don't leave tomorrow you're going to end up really wet and cold."

I watch her body tighten and jerk with my words. Still, she doesn't turn around.

"Goodnight, Mr. Sterling," she says and disappears behind the closing flap of her tent. A minute later I hear the zipper move on the door.

I frown. When she called me Mr. Sterling, all I wanted to do was bend her over my knees and spank her ass.

I warned her. That's all I can do. I wasn't kidding about the tent, nor the rain headed our way. She's going to end up wet, cold and miserable...

Or worse, she doesn't leave and I forget all the reasons I need to stay away from her, and then make sure she's wet, hot and completely filled.... *with me.*

CHAPTER 7

Lexi

It is the crack of thunder that wakes me up. My tent is shaking, the wind howling outside fierce, violent. A droplet of water falls onto my head. I gasp and sit up, seeing rain coming through my cheap tent. This is the one thing I purchased on my own. Everything else I got from Brooks' storage unit. I bought a cheap, yet pretty tent, and now I am paying for it.

I grab my purse and start looking for my car keys. Looks like I am sleeping in my car tonight. And of course, because my luck totally sucks, I can't find the keys.

Of course.

Another flash of lightning causes the interior of my tent to illuminate. Seconds later the thunder booms.

I cry out on instinct then immediately slap a hand over my mouth. What the hell was I thinking coming out here? No way I can last a week.

More lightning and thunder ensues, but because I can't find

my keys I'm stuck. I wrap the blanket around me and put the material over my head, the water now coming through the tent. God, I cannot believe I bought such a shit item.

"Lexi?" I hear Beau's voice right outside my tent, and part of me wants to ignore him, wants to be proud and act like I didn't totally screw this up. "Lexi, buttercup, I know you're getting soaked in there. Come out and get in my tent until the storm goes away."

I'm tempted to say no, but another splash of water seeps through the blanket and onto my head. I start shivering. I grit my teeth, grab my purse, and head out of the tent. Beau is standing on the other side with an umbrella, a grin on his face. Damn, I hate when he's right.

"Come on, sweetheart." He holds his hand out, and even though he pissed me off earlier, I find myself slipping my hand in his much bigger one. He closes his fingers around mine and together we go to his tent.

The rain is really coming down hard, the sound of it beating against the tent almost deafening. His tent is spacious, and as I sit in one corner and watch as he digs around for another lantern he's got in his bag, I can't help but appraise him.

Beau is so attractive, big and strong in that hardworking kind of way. His biceps flex and I feel my body heat. I grow wet between my legs, and my nipples become so hard I'm surprised they don't rip through my T-shirt.

I grab the material and pull it away from my body. The fabric is slightly damp from the rain, and the fact that I'm not wearing a bra just now hits me. I feel my face heat, know I'm probably red as a tomato. I reach for one of his blankets and pull it up to cover my chest just as he faces me. He looks at me for a second, cocks an eyebrow, and a smirk covers his face.

Damn, he either can read me well, or he already saw the outline of my nipples when we first got into the tent. I glance away, not wanting to look at him because some pretty filthy things are running through my head right now.

He doesn't say anything, thankfully, and a second later the tent gets brighter as he turns on the lantern. For long seconds we sit there in silence, and when he starts rifling through his bag again, he produces a dry shirt and a pair of sweats.

"Here." He hands the items over to me. "You're soaked and you'll get sick if you stay in those damp things."

I look at him like he's grown two heads.

He exhales. "Lexi, we're adults. I'll look away if you want, but change out of the damn clothes and don't be stubborn about it."

What I'm really thinking about is getting naked in front of him. So many things have gone through my head over the years, things I imaged—fantasized—about doing with Beau. I want to be his, want his hands on me, his mouth on mine. I want the world to know that he loves me, the same way I love him. But those are just that … fantasies. It's not reality, and I really need to get that through my head.

I don't bother to wait until he turns around. I drop the blanket and lift the shirt above my head. We are adults, as he says, and it's not like he's never seen a pair of breasts before. I could almost chuckle at the shocked way he looks when he sees me getting dressed, before he turns around. When I have the shirt on I go for the pants next. He does turn his head away then and I grin.

"Shit, Lexi," he says under his breath.

Good, it's about time I'm the one making *him* uncomfortable.

CHAPTER 8

Beau

"Something wrong?" she asks. I can hear the laughter in her voice and though she's trying to play innocent, we both know she's trying to tease me. She has no idea what she's doing. If she knew what was inside my head right now, it would scare the fuck out of her. I want her pretty damn badly, especially since the image of her nipples poking through her damp shirt is engrained in my head. Did no one ever teach her she shouldn't poke a damn bear? And I feel pretty feral right now. I have to clench my damn hands to keep them from shaking.

"You should be careful who you flash your tits to, buttercup," I growl, turning around just as she's pulling my jogging pants over her ass. I glance at her once more, seeing her bent over, my gaze now glued to the way the material slides over her tanned, firm hips. Hips that I've dreamed of holding onto, bruising with my fingers as I sink inside her tight little body.

Jesus.

I may not survive tonight. My dick is so hard that my jeans are suffocating the damn thing.

"It's *you,* Beau. We're both adults like you said," she says with just enough sass that I want to smack her hard on the ass and leave my handprint. My dick is dripping; I can feel the pre-cum on the head—that's how fucking close I am to coming. Lexi has no idea what she's playing with.

I move up to her, and I can't stop smiling. My clothes dwarf her. There should be nothing sexy about the way my shirt hangs off of her or how she's holding the material at her waist to keep my sweats on her sweet ass. But I don't think I've seen a woman look better. I reach over and grab a towel I had lying on my cot, and hand it over to her. Then I move my hands down to hold over the one she has clenched, holding her pants on.

"Are you having fun teasing me, Lexi?" I ask, not bothering to hold in the growl that leaves me. I know it's not my imagination when I hear the way her breath rushes from her lips. I grab the waistband of the sweats, her skin warm against my fingers. I begin folding them down, and cinching them to make them tighter against her stomach.

"I think I am," she whispers, and her gaze is clouded with desire. I'd have to be a fool not to see it.

"I'm not a boy like you're used to dealing with, Lexi. I'm a man. You shouldn't tease a man—we might bite back," I warn her and I turn her around gently so her back is to me now.

"I doubt you could dish out anything I couldn't handle, Beau," she says and she's putting on a good front, but her voice is threaded with need and as I move my hand down her back, she shivers—and I'm pretty fucking sure it has nothing to do with the cold.

I move even closer to her, and I let my hands brush against the plush cheeks of her ass before they rest on each of her hips. I'm the one testing her now, seeing how far she'll let me go. My body is against hers now, and when she tries to move away from me, I assert pressure on her, not letting her.

"No," I say in a low rumble that seems to vibrate through me.

"What are you doing, Beau?" she asks, her voice tender.

"I'm just drying your hair, Lexi. That's okay, isn't it?" I whisper against her ear. I have no fucking doubt in my mind she knows I'm not really trying to dry her damn hair.

"I...yeah. That's okay," she answers.

I get the towel and carefully use it to get most of the moisture from the darkened tresses.

"You have beautiful hair, Lexi," I tell her. I shouldn't, but I can't seem to help myself. The same way I push against her ass, wondering if she can feel how full and heavy my cock is—even through my jeans.

"Beau," she moans, pushing her ass against my cock.

I could take her now. Take her and make her mine—the way I should have years ago—the way I was always meant to.

I wrap my hand around her hair and tilt her head back, desire filling my body. I'm on a razor's edge and I'm so tired of holding back.

And then an image of Brooks flashes in my mind.

Brooks. My best friend. The man who saved my ass more than a few times in Kandahar while on patrol. A man who gave me a family when I was younger, when I had none.

I owe him. If nothing else, I owe him loyalty. He doesn't want me with his baby sister. As quick as that, my desire turns to anger.

Anger at Brooks, anger at the situation, and anger at Lexi for teasing me. Most of all I am angry at myself.

"You feel what happens when you tease a real man, Lexi?" I

ask. I pull her body hard against my raging cock. There's no way she can help but feel it now. "You better be careful what you ask for, you just might get it."

I hurl the words at her, doing my best to keep the anger out of them, but instead making them sound like I'm mocking her. It's not easy. It nearly destroys me and my cock is so hard it aches. I gently push her body apart from mine.

She turns to look at me, shock evident on her face.

I do my best to hide the torture I'm in and smile at her, daring her to push me further.

"I hate you," she whispers and that one sentence is enough to wipe the fake smile from my face.

Fuck.

CHAPTER 9

Lexi

I can't sleep, and it has nothing to do with the storm raging outside. Over the last couple of hours the weather has only gotten worse, with the water beating against the tent, the wind shaking it.

I shift so I'm now facing Beau. He's got his back to me, his chest rising and falling underneath a thin blanket over him. His upper back and shoulder are exposed, and I cannot believe he's not chilled not wearing a shirt.

Although I'm not complaining about the view.

The weather outside is pretty cold due to the rain and wind, but inside the tent is nice and warm. It's clear he didn't cheap out on shelter like I did.

He left the lantern turned on, but on a low setting so that there is a dim glow inside the interior. I look at the dips and curves on his bicep, the strength and power that come from him clear. He is so muscular, with the sinew and tendons bunching under his golden skin.

I didn't lie when I said I wasn't teasing him earlier tonight, that I didn't want to get under his skin the way he did with me. But I was angry when he denied me, when he acted like what was going on between us was wrong.

I heard the self-anger in his voice, even though it was clear he tried to hide it. I have a feeling that this all had to do with Brooks. Maybe there is some loyalty there, with Beau feeling he would be crossing lines with my brother if he were with me.

Or maybe all of this is in my head. Maybe he really doesn't want me in the way that I want him.

The latter frustrates me. I felt the evidence of his arousal for me, could see it in the way he looked at me. But he is fighting it, hiding it. Even now I am aroused, my pussy wet, my nipples hard and aching. I wonder if he's actually sleeping, or if he is just as worked up as I am. Because I must be a fool, crazy, or hell, both, I find myself reaching out and running my fingers along his arm. His skin is warm and smooth, and I shiver, wanting to be pressed against him, feel that warmth for myself.

This isn't just about sex. This is about me loving Beau, wanting him in my life as more than what we've been, and praying he feels the same way I do. But I'm so afraid of screwing things up, that being bold, like I was earlier tonight, and teasing him, could ruin what little relationship we really have.

I know he is like a brother to Brooks, that he doesn't want to cross lines and fuck things up there, but I'm a grown woman and I know what I want. I want this man lying right beside me. I want to feel his naked body pressed to mine, keeping me warm, letting me know that I'm not the only one feeling these things. I want things to be more than me poking a sleeping bear with a stick and seeing if I can get a rise out of it.

Something in me opens up and I feel stronger, braver. I won't let this opportunity pass. If it ends up ruining everything, then at least I tried. At least I was able to say I went after what I wanted.

I sit up, the blanket falling from my body and pooling around my waist. I start to sweat despite the chilled air outside this tent, beads forming between my breasts and down the length of my spine. Can he hear how heavy I'm breathing? It sounds like a freight train to me. My pulse is beating in my throat, pounding hard, threating to burst free. Am I really going to do this? What if this all blows up? What if he rejects me?

I have to try.

I slip off the oversized shirt, the one that smells like Beau. My nipples instantly harden further as the air hits them. I start to shiver, but it doesn't have anything to do with being shirtless. I'm nervous, afraid of what's to come, if I'm making the right choice. I shimmy out of the sweats, and soon I'm naked, Beau still facing away from me, my heart beating a mile a minute. I reach out and place my hand on his bicep, his muscles flexing beneath my touch.

"Beau," I say softly, gently. I curl my fingers into his skin a little harder, and he stirs, turning around and facing me. I can see that he wasn't asleep by the wide-eyed look he gives me. Or maybe he's surprised to see me sitting beside him naked. I could have laughed at the latter. Of course he's shocked to see me like this. But I exhale slowly. "I want to cross that line," I say softly. "I love you, have loved you for longer than I want to admit." I swallow the thick lump in my throat.

He doesn't say anything for long seconds, and I'm afraid that this is where he tells me nothing can happen between us. And then he sits up, his chest coming into full view as his blanket slides off of his body.

"Lexi." He says my name in a deep, gruff voice. He reaches out and pushes a stray piece of hair from my cheek, his finger brushing my skin. I shiver. And then he wraps his hand around my waist and hauls me onto his lap. My bare breasts press to his chest, a gasp leaving me. I can feel how hard he is, his dick like a steel pipe between my thighs. "Lexi," he growls, and then he slams his mouth on mine and fucks me with his tongue and lips.

All I can do is wrap my arms around his neck and hold on.

CHAPTER 10

Beau

I shouldn't do this. Fuck, I know I shouldn't, but I'm face to face with every fucking fantasy I've ever had in my life. It would take a stronger man than I've ever met to turn Lexi away. When it comes to her I'm weak as fuck, and I'm tired of pushing her away. I know there will be hell to pay and Brooks will probably kill me, but I can't let her go this time.

I can't.

I devour her mouth and the sweet, smoldering taste of her makes me ache. Her warm, naked body rubs against me, teasing my dick. I've fantasized about her for years, but nothing ever came close to how this feels.

I move my hands down her body, memorizing the feel of her under my touch. It feels as if she's branding me, but, hell, she branded me a long time ago. It's always been Lexi... *Always.*

Lexi is grinding her ass against my hard cock, torturing me, and I doubt she has a clue. If she doesn't stop, I'm going to come in my pants and that's not how I want tonight to go. I break away from her, standing us both up. Thank fuck the tent is massive and we have plenty of room for what I have planned. Her eyes glow right now; there's so much desire and emotion in them, they captivate me.

"Lay down for me, Lexi," I order, my voice vibrating with the hunger I feel as I squeeze her breasts in my hands.

This is it. The moment I expect Lexi to falter, to run away. I half expect her to. I've not given her the soft words that she deserves. I can't, not yet. I have to hold myself back. Maybe because I expect this all to blow up soon. Why would she pick me to spend forever with? She wouldn't. She may want me right now, but Lexi is too good for me, too special. She deserves the best. Not a broken down ex-soldier with nothing on the horizon. When Brooks finds out, it will fall apart. She will push me aside under Brooks' demands. She's always done what her big brother wanted. Brooks knows and I know that I don't deserve Lexi, but I can't stop myself from taking the gift she's giving me now.

Her big eyes look up at me, so raw and full of love my gut clenches. She's perfect in every way.

"Like this?" she whispers as she lowers herself on the bed. She lays down on the sleeping bag, her hands covering her breasts.

"Spread your legs for me, Lexi. Show me your pussy," I order, hypnotized by her.

She bends her legs and holds them apart, her feet flat on the ground. A fine blush runs over her entire body and I can see she's embarrassed, but she still gives me what I want. I ache at how innocent she looks. I wish I hadn't pushed her away all those years. I lost my chance to be her first, to be the man who claimed her virginity. Her first… It's for the best that didn't happen. If I had claimed her back then, I would have been her first and her last. There's no way I would have let her get away from me. Still, it hurts me that she was with a man who didn't deserve her. I'm glad she kicked him to the curb.

I mourn the loss of tasting her innocence, but if she was a virgin I couldn't have her. That would make her completely off limits. At least this way I can have her...until reality intrudes and she pushes me away.

"Touch yourself for me, Lexi," I order, pushing her further—testing her limits. I slide my pants down, my dick so hard it hurts. I step out of them and wrap my hand around my cock, stroking it as I look down at her.

"Oh... God," she gasps, her focus on my dick. She moves her hand down her stomach to her pussy. I watch its path, every perfect fucking inch, and my cock weeps for her. A large drop of cum drips off the head and slides down the shaft. I stroke myself as Lexi clumsily touches her pussy. She's nervous. I smile, liking that I'm pushing her to her limits. "Maybe we shouldn't... I'm not sure you'll..."

"I'll what?" Just knowing what she was about to say turns me on even more. "Trust me Lexi, I'll definitely make you feel good," I tell her, not about to let her back out now. I'm too far gone. If she wasn't sure she should have never offered me a glimpse of heaven.

I get down on my knees between her legs and move my cock against her entrance, her juices sliding against my dick, the heat of her pussy beckoning me. She's so fucking wet and I've not touched her yet. How good will she feel when I finally get inside? I lean over and suck one of her tight nipples between my teeth, biting gently and using my tongue to tease it. Lexi's body jerks in response, her nails biting into my neck as she tries to hold on to me. She jerks under me, her hips thrusting and causing the lips of her pussy to wrap around my cock. It feels so fucking good. I suck hard on her nipple while pinching the other one. I'm rewarded with her cry of pleasure as her back bows up off the sleeping bag.

She's so fucking responsive.

"See, Lexi? There's no going back. I'm going to make you feel good," I vow, still teasing her tits with my hands, while she desperately grinds her clit against the shaft of my cock, trying to make herself come.

"I didn't mean that," she gasps, pushing against me, trying to her body closer to mine. "It's just you're so big," she adds, as another shiver rolls through her body.

Damn, if I wait much longer she's going to come like this. I have to get inside of her.

"Play with your tits, Lexi. I want to watch as I fuck you," I order, taking her hands from my neck and putting them on her breasts. She does what I ask, her chest heaving up and down as she pulls on her nipples. I can tell she's so fucking close to exploding. Jesus.

I wrap my hand around my dick, using the tip to tease her swollen clit, pressing it against her.

"Oh God, that feels so good, Beau," she whimpers. Her hands are almost violent on her tits now. She's lost to passion in a way I never expected.

"You don't have to worry, baby. My cock will fit inside of you and it's going to make you feel so good," I tell her, dragging my dick through her sweet juices and positioning myself at her opening.

"You will?" she breathes.

"Look at me, Lexi," I order. She brings her pleasure-filled gaze to me. "I will, honey. You keep your eyes on me. I want to see you when I get inside your pussy. I want to see your face as I claim you."

"O-okay, Beau," she whispers, her voice thick from her lust.

"You're so fucking perfect, Lexi. You're everything. I'm going to give you so much pleasure, you'll forget you ever had a man before me," I growl right before I thrust deep inside of her.

"But, there's never been anyone else," she cries as I thrust my cock in. "I've never wanted anyone but you," she adds as I seat myself deep inside of her. Her body is rigid, her eyes wide, her mouth parted. Shit. She didn't need to tell me. I felt it as soon as I thrust in her body. I am Lexi's first. I'm the first man to claim her.

She's a virgin.

And I just took her cherry like a wild man. Fuck, I know I hurt her. I do my best to hold perfectly still, mentally beating myself up, but all I can think is I'm Lexi's first and I'll be her fucking last.

She's mine.

CHAPTER 11

Lexi

I can't breathe, can't even speak. The pain, burning, and stretching is unlike anything I've ever felt before. But that discomfort doesn't take away from the immense pleasure I feel. I am wet, achingly so. My nipples are hard, erect, and tingling. And the fact Beau is above me, his dick thrust deep inside of me, claiming my virginity, pushes everything else to the back.

I can see by his expression he's startled to realize I am a virgin. I hadn't wanted to tell him because I hadn't wanted to ruin things. Would he have said no if he knew he would be my first? *I want him to be my only.*

"Fuck, Lexi, baby." His voice is deep, harsh, guttural. His entire body is tense, his muscles contracting and relaxing underneath his golden skin. "You should've told me this was your first time. I wouldn't have been a fucking madman thrusting into you." His jaw is tight, the muscle underneath the skin flexing. I can see how he's trying to rein in his control, how he's trying not to break. And even though it's uncomfortable, and the pain is there, I've waited for this moment for too long. I'm not about to stop it.

"I won't break," I finally say, forcing myself to relax. It takes some long seconds before he finally relaxes as well. "Fuck me, Beau." I watch as he shifts, changes. My words have done something to him; have his control slipping. He groans and then starts moving inside of me, back and forth, in and out.

He's slow at first, his motions easy, maybe trying to get me adjusted. But the pleasure increases, the pain diminishing. I arch my back, my breasts thrusting up. I make a long, drawn-out cry. That seems to be his breaking point. He grabs my hands and brings them above my head, holding my wrists, his fingers wrapping gently around my skin. And then he starts really pounding into me, faster and harder, the sound of wet skin slapping together filling the tent.

I'm breathing so hard, sweat starting to blossom over me. I lift my head slightly and look down the length of my body, seeing his six-pack flexing as he thrusts in and out of me. The rain has let up slightly, but I can still hear the patter of droplets on the tent. The light from the lantern glows within the interior, and as he pulls out I can see the glossiness of my arousal coating his shaft. I also see streaks of blood, the product of my virginity taken, given to Beau.

"Lexi, fuck, baby." His eyes are closed, his jaw set tight. He doesn't have a hold on my wrists any longer, but his hands are still by my head, his fingers digging into the sleeping bag. The sound it makes as the nylon crinkles underneath his fingers fills my head.

He pulls out of me before I can even comprehend what's happening. He's on his back, has me over him, my legs on either side of his waist. I feel the stiff length of his erection pressed between my thighs, both of our breathing heavy, hard.

"Grab hold of my cock, Lexi," he says on demand. "Put it inside of you, baby."

I do as he says, reaching between our bodies and wrapping my finger around the thick root of his dick. He's so big, so thick that my fingers don't touch when I hold him. And then I place the tip at my entrance and slowly sink down on his length. We both groan, and tingles race along my arms and legs. He fills me to the brink, making me feel as though I'm going to split into two.

"Now ride me, Lexi. Fuck yourself on me until you come. I want to watch the pleasure wash over your face."

His words nearly have me climaxing as it is. I start bouncing up and down on him, my breasts shaking from the motion. I force my eyes to stay open so I can stare at Beau and see the pleasure on his face, as well.

Up and down. Faster. Harder. Finally I can't keep my eyes open any longer. I tilt my head back as ecstasy washes through me. I cry as I come, my pussy clenching around his thick cock, needing him deeper inside of me. It's only a second later that I hear Beau groaning out as well. He has his hands on my waist, his fingers digging into my skin. I know there'll be bruises in the morning, but I anticipate them, want to see them covering my flesh.

It'll be a mark of ownership.

He comes inside of me, filling me with his seed.

"That's it," he says in broken words. "Milk my cock; suck all the cum out."

The pleasure is never ending, and I absorb it all. It feels even more incredible because I'm with the man I love, the one person I've wanted for as long as I can remember.

When the pleasure diminishes and I can no longer hold myself up, I collapse on his chest. For a second I wonder if he'll push me off, say this was a mistake, that we should've never done this. But instead he wraps his arms around me and just holds me for long minutes. Then he rolls us so we're facing each other on our sides, lifts his hand, and pushes a strand of my hair away from my face. He looks into my eyes and I can see that he cares for me, that this wasn't a mistake. What we shared was perfect.

"You're mine."

Yes I am.

CHAPTER 12

Beau

"What are you doing?" Lexi asks from the zippered opening of the tent.

She looks so fucking good this morning my dick aches, the remembrance of what we did last night like a brand in my fucking marrow. Her hair is all rumpled and she has it pulled up in a messy bun. She doesn't have a stitch of makeup on, but then Lexi never needs makeup. She's naturally beautiful, inside and out. Her lips are bruised from our night of lovemaking, swollen, red and unbelievably sexy. I imagine them sliding down on my cock and the semi-hard-on that I've been sporting all morning instantly turns into a raging erection. I should be fucking worried when a woman's lips can make my dick hard enough to drive nails into concrete. She's not just any woman, though. She's Lexi and she's always owned my heart.

She's always been mine.

"Fixing you some breakfast," I tell her with a smile. "Come over here and give your man a kiss."

I watch as she walks gingerly toward me. She's obviously still sore and tender from our lovemaking last night, which I fucking like—even if that does make me a bastard. Possessiveness slams into me knowing that I claimed her, that my cock is the only one that's ever known how hot and wet, how fucking tight she is. *I'm the only one who will ever know what she feels like.*

"Are you my man?" she asks, her eyes wide, and despite what we shared last night, innocent.

"Definitely, sweetheart and the only one you'll ever have."

"Really?"

"I'm not letting another man have you, Lexi. You're mine now. You gave that to me last night, and I'm not letting you go."

"I like the sound of that," she says softly and wraps her arms around me.

"I do too, baby. I do too."

I hold her close for a few minutes, breathing in her scent, and just let the fact that I have her in my arms soothe me. For so long, I've felt like there has been half of me missing. Now I realize that it's not been the military, or any of that shit. It's been Lexi. She's been mine since that first kiss, I've just been running from it. That's over. Brooks isn't going to like it, but I don't give a fuck. He can get the hell over it.

"That does smell good," she says and I grin.

It's a simple breakfast. Toast, eggs and bacon, but I like that I'm taking care of Lexi. I always want to do that. She deserves a man who will put her first, and I want to be that for her.

"Go back inside the tent, relax and stay warm, and I'll bring you a plate."

"I'd rather eat out here, around the fire," she says, surprising me.

"You aren't cold?"

"I've got my sweater on and besides, it feels good. I love the smell of the fresh air. It's exactly why I came out here."

"If you're sure," I hedge.

"I am, but you don't have to do everything. I can help."

"I want to take care of my girl. Is that a crime?" I ask her with a wink, putting the food on the plates.

"Beau, if you only knew how long I've been dying to hear you call me your girl," she laughs as she sits down. "To be honest, it's kind of surreal to hear you say it now."

"Get used to it, sweetheart. I'll be saying it often," I tell her and hand her a plate of food. I just stare at her, unable to believe that this is reality right now. I feel good, really fucking good.

"If it's a dream, do me a favor and don't wake me."

"I hope it's a good dream at least," I joke, suddenly jealous of the bacon she's eating as it slips between her lips. I reach down and adjust my dick before the bastard bursts through my jeans.

"The best."

I clear my throat and do my best to pull my gaze away from her eating. If I don't I'm going to fuck her right here in front of the tent and I'm not sure her body is ready for that. I tried to be gentle with her last night, but she's way too tender for what my dick is demanding.

"Not everyone will be happy about the two of us," I tell her, tackling the one issue that is worrying me.

"You mean Brooks, don't you?" She doesn't state it like a question.

"Yeah, honey. He doesn't want me with you. He's made that clear over the years."

She shakes her head. "That's crazy. You're his best friend. He has to know the kind of man you are. You'd never hurt me." She scowls. "Besides, I'm an adult, and I know what I want." She looks me in the eyes.

I love that Lexi only sees the best in me. I want to tell her that Brooks knows I've not always been the best kind of man. I've fucked up a lot in my life. The thing is, I was always running away from Lexi and my love for her, knowing I wasn't what Brooks wanted for his little sister.

I don't tell her that, however. I don't want to dim the picture of me she has in her head. I'm going to fight like hell to live up to that image. I want to be a good man. I want to be a man that Lexi can be proud of.

"You're his little sister, honey," I say instead. "He's just protecting you."

"He'll just have to get happy or get sad," she grumbles and she looks so cute I laugh.

"What does that even mean?" I ask, shaking my head.

"It means that I'm not giving you up, Beau. I don't care what Brooks or anyone else says."

"Is that a fact?" I ask her, feeling more at ease than I've felt in years.

"Damn skippy," she says as she sucks bacon grease from her fingers.

As much as I want to laugh at her use of words, my gaze is drawn to the way her lips suck on her finger. She's not doing it to be sexy; it's completely just Lexi being natural, and maybe that makes it even hotter.

"Sweetheart, if you don't quit sucking on your fingers like that, we're going to have problems," I warn her, my voice hoarse.

"We are?" she asks, instantly stopping what she's doing and watching me closely. "Like what?"

"Like I'm going to give you something else to suck on," I mutter, adjusting my cock again.

Lexi puts her plate on the ground beside her and comes over to me. I don't say anything; I just wait to see what she does. It doesn't take long. She drops to her knees in front of me.

"Give me something else to suck on, Beau. I dare you," she whispers, her voice thick with desire and fuck, I'm lost to her.

Completely and utterly lost.

CHAPTER 13

Lexi

I follow Beau up the trail, beads of sweat dotting between my breasts and the length of my spine. The ground is damp from the storm last night, the leaves sticking to my shoes. I straighten, pushing past the burning in my thighs and the ache in my feet. He looks over his shoulder at me and grins. I know he can see how this seemingly easy hike is a pain in the ass for me by the look on his face. But I keep my mouth shut and trek on.

Apparently this isn't the first time Beau has been camping up here by himself. And when he said he wanted to show me something special, I hadn't even thought of denying him.

"How are you doing back there, baby girl?"

I can't help the blush that no doubt steals over my body at the endearment he calls me. "I'm good." I give him two thumbs up and he grins and gives me a wink.

When he turns back around and starts walking, I brace both of my hands on my thighs and lean forward, huffing and puffing. Sweat is dotting my forehead now, and I realize how out of shape I am. I see him start to turn to look at me again and I straighten and follow him up the path like I'm not dying inside.

"Just a little bit farther," he says and gives me another straight, white-toothed grin.

We only walk for another five minutes or so before I see where he's taking me. I take off my backpack and set it beside me, bracing my hands on my hips as I stare out at the lake. The sun is high in the sky, glistening off the water, making it look like it is sprinkled with glitter. Large pine trees surround the lake, and I can see water lapping at the shore.

"It's beautiful," I look over at Beau and see he's watching me, this longing expression on his face. "Thank you for bringing me here," I say and smile.

"It's almost as beautiful as you are."

Any other time, and from any other guy, I would've thought it was a clichéd saying, but hearing Beau say it to me makes me feel pretty damn special.

He is in front of me a second later, his hands on my waist, pulling me closer to him. My breasts press against his chest. I feel his body heat through our clothes and instantly become wet. Even though I am sore from last night, I want him.

I lift my arms and wrap them around his neck, rising on my toes and pressing my lips to his. I don't think about anything else except showing Beau how much I care for him, how much I love him.

He gives me a small kiss on the lips, but before anything can become hotter he takes a step back, to my disappointment. And then, surprising me, he starts undressing. Before I know it he is naked, his erection prominent. He gives me a half smirk and I feel my heart flutter.

He is big and strong, with muscles that are defined, and with boyish good looks that make him seem like he's not the bad boy I know he is. It's that rebellious streak that I love.

"Go on, baby. Get undressed so we can see how cold the water is."

Although it stormed last night, the air is surprisingly warm. But I have doubts on if the water matches that. I know that shit is probably ice cold. I look over at the lake, and although it looks beautiful, the truth is I don't care how cold it is. It can be freezing and I'll still want to go in with Beau.

I turn back toward him and smile, quickly undressing myself.

Before I know what he is doing, Beau is in front of me again, his arms wrapped around my body, and he easily lifts me as if I weigh nothing. He has us in the water seconds later. I scream out, the chill so sudden that my entire body tenses.

I can hear him laughing, and I push away from him, scowling. He splashes water at me and I sputter as it hits me in the face. I can't help but laugh in return. For the next ten minutes we do nothing but swim around, occasionally splashing each other, but overall just having a fun time. I can't remember the last time I felt so free, so happy.

Beau is in front of me and pulls me close to his body. His body heat seeps into mine and I sigh, wrapping my arms around his shoulders and my legs around his waist. I can feel how hard he is, his erection pressing right between my legs.

"I'm never letting you go," he says softly right beside my ear. I close my eyes and rest my head on his shoulder.

"I don't want you to."

CHAPTER 14

Beau

The ride back home is quiet. Lexi is obviously as lost in her thoughts as I am mine. I'm nervous as fucking hell, to be honest. Everything was perfect on the mountain. Lexi was mine and nothing else mattered.

What happens now?

Will Lexi still be proud to call me hers once we get back to reality? Her family will never think I'm good enough for her. Fuck, it's probably a good thing Brooks is still overseas. If he were here he'd no doubt kill me for just knowing I looked at Lexi the "wrong way." I'm not exactly the high-class type of man her friends mess with either. Will Lexi be ashamed of me?

I need to quit being a damn pussy and just talk to her. You would think I've lost my balls. I pull into Lexi's drive, shut the engine off and just stare at her garage door. I undo my seatbelt and from the sounds, I can hear Lexi doing the same. Still, neither of us talk for long moments. Lexi is finally the first to break the silence.

"I'm sorry about my car. I didn't mean to be a problem for you," she murmurs.

"It's not your fault you had a flat, baby girl. You really do need to always have a spare, though. What if you had been out alone? There's no cellphone signal up there." Shit. I sound grouchy as hell. It's just that the thought of her being stranded in the middle of nowhere scares the hell out of me. She needs to be more careful. "Besides, I wanted to drive you."

"You don't really seem like it, Beau. Has something changed?"

I turn to look at her—*really* look at her. That's when I see the same fear on her face that I'm feeling, and I feel like a chump. I turn into her, pulling her up on my lap—which isn't easy because of the steering wheel, but I manage.

"Absolutely nothing has changed for me, Lexi. I'm actually more worried about you changing your mind. Things might look different for you here than they did on the mountain, when it was just the two of us," I confess. I gently tangle my fingers in her hair, holding her head back so she looks me in the eyes, so she knows I'm fucking serious. Her pulse beats against my palm. That, combined with the feel of her warm skin, seems to center me.

"You're being silly, Beau. I've loved you for years, even when you barely spoke to me. Do you really think that would change now that we're together?" she whispers softly. I wrap my arms around her body, pulling her in closer. I close my eyes, breathing her scent in.

"I've been a fool, a stupid fool," I groan.

She pulls back to look at me, her beautiful face smiling and, as hokey as it sounds, it's like the stars have been captured in her eyes. She's so beautiful... *she's everything.*

"I know how you can make it up to me, Beau," she says with a naughty little smile and a blush that makes my dick push against the zipper of my jeans.

"How's that?"

"Stay with me tonight. Don't leave."

"What about your car?"

"We can go get it tomorrow, or I'll send Triple A. Right now the only thing I want is you in my bed and…"

"Say it, Lexi," I order roughly, my hand palming her breast as her body rocks teasingly against me.

"I want you in my bed, Beau. I want you inside of me, all night. I want to fall asleep with you inside of me."

"Fuck, baby girl…" I growl, the images of what she's describing enough to drive me to my knees.

"Please, Beau? I've waited so long for you, I don't want to spend any time apart," she says, laying her heart out for me to see. She gave me her body, but this is something else entirely.

I don't know how I manage it. I couldn't begin to explain it, but somehow we make it out of the truck, me kissing her and barely taking time to breathe. We even manage to make it through the front door and down the hall to her bedroom.

I have to have her, all of her.

Now. Hard. Fast. Urgently.

CHAPTER 15

Beau

I pull Lexi in closer, her naked body so warm, so soft and feminine against mine. I just got done making love to her, fucking her until she couldn't even breathe. And only when she came three times for me did I finally find my own release.

Now, after the pleasure has diminished, just holding her is perfection. I run my hand over her flat belly, thinking about my child growing inside of her. I want that. I want her as my wife, by my side forever. But I don't want to say any of that yet, don't want to freak her out. I don't want her running from me, from us.

We are meant to be together, and it is just a damn shame it took this long for it to happen. I close my eyes and bury my face against her hair, inhaling deeply. She smells sweet, like flowers and a hint of vanilla.

I feel her stir, her soft, breathy moan causing my cock to come to attention again. The fucker is sore from being buried deep in her these last two days, but hell, I can go all fucking night if she wants me to.

"How about I give you something to put a smile back on your face?" She moans in response, and I rise up to look down at her. She turns and faces me slightly, her sleepy smile making my cock jerk again. "You want me to wake you up, baby?"

She grins now and nods, not saying anything.

I move down her body, pulling the covers up over me. She already has her legs spread, her pussy smelling so fucking sweet. I want to get drunk off of her, off of her flavor. I don't bother waiting, don't even try and control myself. I place my hands on her inner thighs, pushing them open even farther, and devour her. I suck and lick at her folds, take her little clit into my mouth and run my tongue around it. She's panting above me, her hands under the sheets and tangled in my hair.

I feast on her, sucking her clit even harder, needing her to get off for me, to climax against my lip and tongue.

"I'm so close," she breathes out harshly and I renew my efforts. I pull her pussy lips apart with my thumbs and lick her slit from her pussy hole right back up to her little nub.

And then she comes for me. Her thighs close in around my head, holding me there as I eat her out. I'm dry humping the mattress, my cock hard as steel again. When she relaxes on the bed I climb up her body, my cock pressing right at the center of her. I'm about to push in deep, claim her once more, when I hear a door open and close in the house.

We both stare at each other, confusion clear on Lexi's face.

"You expecting someone?"

She shakes her head and I glance at her closed bedroom door.

"Alexandria?"

Oh. Fuck.

Everything in my body tenses, freezes. The sound of Brooks calling out for Lexi shocks me to my core. It's not so much the fact that I'm lying in bed naked with his sister, about to have my cock balls deep inside her, but the fact he was overseas last I heard.

"Oh my God. Is that Brooks?" she whispers.

"Lexi?" Brooks shouts again.

"Lexi, baby, I think we got trouble." I'm not afraid of being honest with Brooks. I am more worried about how he'll handle me telling him I love Lexi and I'm not going anywhere.

"Shit. He'll flip if he sees us like this." I get off of her and she rushes to get dressed. I, on the other hand, take my time. I have my jeans pulled up, the button undone, the zipper down, when Brooks knocks on the door.

"Alexandria? You in there?"

Lexi looks at me with these big eyes, anxiety clear on her face.

"Ugh, yup. Be right out." She hurries and puts her shirt on. "What are you doing here anyway?" Her voice is high-pitched, and I know Brooks can probably sense there's something going on.

"Are you okay?" he asks. "You sound weird."

I stand up, walk over to her, and kiss her on the mouth, hoping to calm her down.

"I'm fine," she finally says, her voice softer. I give her a smile, help her with her shirt, and finish getting dressed. Then I go to her bedroom door, open it, and face Brooks. I know shit's about to hit the fan, but hell, I'm ready. I've been ready for a long fucking time.

CHAPTER 16

Beau

"What the hell is going on here?" Brooks asks.

I ignore him for a minute, pulling Lexi to my side as I show her through the door and using my body to keep Brooks away from her. I know he won't hurt her, but I don't give a damn if he is her brother. Lexi is mine and I just made her come. Her pussy is wet with her climax and she's my woman. No one but me gets close to her—especially when she's like that.

"What are you doing here, Brooks? I thought you were overseas. Oh my God! Were you hurt? Are you okay?" Lexi asks, trying to push me to the side to get to her brother.

"I'm fine, little sister. I'm on medical leave for a bit," Brooks says to Lexi, but he's glaring at me. There are a lot of unspoken questions on his face.

"Medical leave? What the hell for?" I ask, knowing full well they don't just pass those out.

"That's not important right now, asshole. What's important is you tell me what the fuck you're doing in my sister's bedroom, half dressed?"

"Brooks, it's not what it looks like," Lexi interjects, trying to move between us. I smirk at her response. I can't help it. I move her behind me. The day I hide behind my woman is the day they need to just go ahead and chop off my balls.

"Really sis? Because it looks like Beau has had his dick in you!"

I hear Lexi's gasp and then her muttered, "I guess it kind of is what it looks like," and any other time I might find that funny—but not right now.

I punch him hard in the face for saying that crude shit to my woman. Sister or not, he needs to watch his mouth. Brooks is a big asshole, but I'm just as big and I'm pissed as hell. He falls back, hard. I hear Lexi cry out, but I keep my eye on Brooks.

"You will not disrespect my woman like that," I growl, rubbing my fist because fuck, it hurts. I hit him that hard.

"Damn it, Beau. You didn't have to hit him," Lexi chastises me and pushes past me to move down the hall. I hear water running and look over my shoulder to see her wetting a cloth in the kitchen sink. She brings it to Brooks and he takes it from her, still staring at me. To prove I really am an asshole, I reach down and grab Lexi's hand and pull her away from Brooks. He might be her brother, but I don't want her touching another man right now and helping him.

I'm feeling as possessive as hell right now. My woman's hair is still messed up from being in bed. I know she's wet, and I know how her hands feel. Brooks is as safe as any bastard around her. He's her brother, for Christ's sake. I still don't want him near her.

"What is wrong with you?" Lexi growls, swatting at my arm and trying to go to her brother.

"You don't need to help him," I grumble, trying not to tell her the complete reason and sound like the asshole I am.

"Of course I do! You hit him!"

"He deserved it and you're mine. I hurt my hand, you can see to that," I grumble.

"You hurt your hand?" she asks, sounding shocked.

"Your brother's face is hard." I shrug.

"You want me to ignore my brother's bleeding lip, just to doctor your hand because it's sore from hitting him?" Lexi asks and, put like that, it probably sounds as bad as it is, but I don't care.

"You're my girl. You're supposed to see to me," I mutter.

"Holy shit," Brooks mutters, standing up.

"Shut up," I growl at him, because I can see the understanding in his face.

"You love my sister."

"Brooks, we've just started dating and I really don't think it's your place—"

"Call it like it is, Sis. You've just started fucking."

"Asshole! I told you to keep your tone civil when it came to Lexi," I yell, and I'm getting ready to hit him again when he starts laughing.

"You're completely gone on her. You sad sack. When the hell did this happen?"

"I've loved her for years; you were just too busy demanding I stay away from her to realize it."

"Doesn't look like you've stayed away from her at all from where I'm standing," he replies.

"Because I'm not—not anymore, Brooks. You can get sad or get glad about it. I don't give a fuck, but I'm not letting Lexi go," I tell him, throwing it down. Lexi curls into my side, holding me close.

"Beau," she whispers, pressing a kiss to the side of my neck.

"Well, hell," Brooks says, looking at the two of us.

"I love her, Brooks. I'm going to marry her. I'm going to raise a family with her and I will kill myself every damn day to make sure she never wants for anything."

"Beau, honey. I think I'm the one you're supposed to tell that stuff too," Lexi says softly. I turn my head to look at her. She's smiling and there are tears in her eyes. She's never been more beautiful to me.

"I will tell you, but your brother needs to know this shit, Lexi. I'm not playing here. I'm keeping you, sweetheart. This time, I will not give you up. I want it all with you."

"Even babies," she whispers, proving she heard my speech to her brother.

"Definitely babies," I agree, closing my eyes when she kisses me.

"I can't wait to have your son, Beau."

"It might be a girl, you know—one as beautiful as her mother."

"Jesus. Will you stop getting wood over my sister? At least while I'm here."

I laugh when Lexi's face heats and reach down and adjust myself.

"It might be easier to tell the sun to stop shining, brother," I sigh, giving him the God's honest truth.

"I'm going to need some coffee if I have to handle this crap," Brooks complains.

"Grab a seat at the table and I'll fix us some," Lexi says, giving me a quick kiss on my lips.

"You all right, brother?" I ask Brooks when Lexi leaves and we walk to the table together.

"Fuck off. You always did hit like a girl," he mutters.

"It was strong enough to knock you on your ass," I remind him.

We sit down and stare at each other a moment. I don't see anger on his face anymore. Unless I'm wrong, I think he's good with this. If I knew he was going to take it this well, I never would have run from Lexi like I did.

"You and my kid sister," he says, shaking his head.

"I love her, Brooks. I know I'm not good enough for her, but I meant what I said. I'm going to bust my ass to make sure she never regrets loving me."

"How the hell did this happen?" he asks as the smell of coffee starts to permeate the room. I feel Lexi's arms go around me and loop lazily at my neck. Her breasts push against my head. Happiness fills me. My woman and my best friend and this time… I get to keep Lexi. This time I don't have to rip out my heart and send her away. This time, she is mine. I bring my hand up and lay it over hers, feeling for the first time in my life like everything is exactly the way it is supposed to be.

"That's easy, Brooks," Lexi says.

"Easy?" he asks.

"Definitely. We went camping together and I impressed him with just how well I could pitch his tent."

"Jesus," Brooks growls, his fist hitting the table.

"I can't believe you just said that, Lexi," I laugh, looking up at her.

"What? Are you saying you don't like the way I handled your tent pole?"

"And I'm out of here," Brooks growls, getting up from the table.

"Wait! Where are you going?" Lexi asks Brooks, laughing.

"Away from here," he answers, opening the door.

"But, I was just about to tell you how much fun Beau and I had when we—"

"La-la-la-la! I can't hear you," Brooks grumbles, slamming the door behind him. Lexi starts laughing, and I stand up and pull her into my arms.

"I can't believe you just did that," I whisper, shaking my head. My hands travel down to her ass, holding her and pressing her against my hard cock.

"I wanted him gone," she confesses, her hands pushing at my pants.

"Why's that, baby girl?" I moan as she wraps her hand around my cock, squeezing it firmly in her hand.

"You told me you were giving me babies. I've decided I want them now."

"Is that a fact?"

"Definitely."

"I guess I better get started, then."

"I couldn't agree more," she says before I take her lips in a kiss.

It's a kiss full of love, of happiness and promise, and everything good. Because that's what Lexi is.

She's everything.

EPILOGUE

Lexi

One year later

I sit on the couch, my shirt pulled up, the bottle of lotion right beside me. I pump a few dollops into my palm and rub my hands together before smoothing lotion over my round belly. I've long since removed my wedding ring, my finger too swollen to have it comfortably on. But I can't help but smile at that fact. Since being with Beau, it seems like everything just fell into place. We dated, got to know each other on a level that wasn't because I was Brooks' little sister, or because we were friends.

And even though we haven't used protection since that night camping, I didn't get pregnant until now. I suppose things just have a way of working out.

We really got to know each other in the way that two people who love each other are supposed to.

He officially proposed a few months after that camping trip, surprising the hell out of me and making me cry big, fat, ugly tears.

I didn't even hesitate in saying yes.

We were married a couple months after that, the wedding intimate. It might have been done fast, but it was beautiful and perfect. It was exactly how I'd always envisioned it.

Beau is the only man I've ever wanted, the only one I've ever loved. After the confrontation with him and my brother, everything was settled. We made it clear that we would do what we wanted, because we were grown-ass adults and we cared about each other. That's all it really took, and Brooks was happy for us. Sure, it was strange for him at first, seeing his best friend and his sister together. But he got used to it, because he didn't have a choice. And when we were married, Brooks was Beau's best man. I loved seeing my brother standing at the altar behind my soon-to-be-husband.

And I love that I am carrying Beau's child. I look down at my belly and smile. I am eight months, huge as a house, but I've never felt prettier. Beau ensures that. Every day he tells me how beautiful I am, rubbing my belly, talking to our child ... little girl. Hell, when we found out the sex of the baby he said he's buying stock in guns and ammunition to ward off any "assholes" who come knocking to date his little girl.

I laughed so hard.

The sound of Beau pulling into the driveway has my heart beating faster. Even after a year of being together I still get the same reaction when he's near, when I know I'm going to see him. He's out of his truck and in the house before I can even get off the couch. But in my defense, at eight months pregnant it's pretty hard doing the latter.

"Baby?" he calls out. I'm sitting on the edge of the couch, staring at the living room entrance when he walks in.

"I'm here, stuck on the couch." I laugh softly.

He grins from ear to ear and is by me a second later, helping me up and pulling me in for an embrace. He leans back and instantly has his hand on my belly, rubbing small circles.

"How you feeling today, baby?" He cups my face with his hands and leans down to kiss me. He holds me close to him, making me feel like I'm the only person in the entire world that matters.

I am.

"Tired, but I'm good," I say, my hand on my lower back, the ache constant. But honestly, all the little twinges and pains that I feel during this pregnancy are worth it. I know the end result will be miraculous.

"Here, sit down and rest, put your feet up. I have something for you." He gets me in the position that he approves of and I can't help but chuckle. But he's gone before I can say anything. A few moments later he returns with a big bundle of roses. I know my face probably lights up. I can feel it.

I'm not surprised he brought me flowers, though, because that is the type of man Beau is. In fact, he gives me flowers seemingly every week. He is a good guy, will fight anyone who tries to hurt me, and I know, without a doubt, he will be an incredible father.

He sets the flowers on the coffee table and sits beside me on the couch. Then he wraps his arm around my shoulder and pulls me in close, kissing the top of my head. For long seconds we don't say anything, the quiet calming, the feeling of sitting next to my husband bringing me more joy than I can even put into words.

"Do you know how much I love you?" he finally says and I shift so I can look up at him. He's already looking at me, his blue eyes so bright, so full of love. "Do you know I would do anything for you?"

I smile and lift my hand to cup his scruff-covered cheek. I smooth my thumb over his cheekbone, loving this man more every day. "Probably as much as I love you?" I raise an eyebrow and grin. He leans down and kisses the tip of my nose, his hand on my belly again. I tip my head back so our mouths meet, and for long moments we kiss, our tongues moving along each other, our breathing increasing. Just then the baby decides to kick something fierce. I gasp and Beau chuckles. We break apart and both look down at my belly.

"With moves like that she'll be a fighter."

I look up at him and smile. "She'll be able to kick guys' asses so you don't have to."

He sobers and shakes his head. "Hell no. Any little punks come asking her out they have to deal with me."

I close my eyes and rest my head on his shoulder, laughing. "Daddy's girl for sure."

"Damn right she will be."

God, this life is perfection, and it is so damn addicting.

Once long ago I saw Beau and knew in my heart that I wanted him to be mine and I wanted to be his... *forever*.

And now... we are. We are exactly that and I couldn't be happier.

The End

Bought and Paid For
Ride My Beard
Planting His Seed
Jingle My Balls
Pitch His Tent

Where to find the Jordan:

Facebook
Newsletter
Pinterest
Twitter
Goodreads
Website

Where to find the Jenika:

Facebook
Newsletter
Instagram
Twitter
Webpage
Goodreads

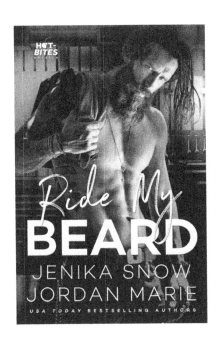

Lola

I grab two beers and set them on my tray, turn, and walk toward the table, moving around horny, drunken guys as they try to grab my ass. But this is the norm at the bar where I work.

The Bottom of the Barrel, which name is pretty accurate for the customers who show up here, is busy as usual. If I didn't need the money, and wasn't always guaranteed a handful of tips at the end of the night—mainly because the guys think I'm sleazy and roll that way—I'd walk away from this place and never look back.

But as it is, the shitty town I live in doesn't have very many options of employment, especially for an eighteen-year-old with a family that has made sure everyone views her as trailer-park trash.

A mother who has a steady number of random men rolling

EXCERPT: RIDE MY BEARD

between her sheets and a father who only sees me as a one-night-stand mistake. This is the life that has always been my constant.

The music is loud, the jukebox in the corner older than I am. It's got buttons missing and a few songs skip constantly. But for the crowd that comes into the bar it's good enough.

The only thing they care about is slinging back cheap drinks, getting lap dances from the loose women who hang around town, and asking me for fifty-dollar blowjobs after my shift like I'll finally give in and do it one of these nights.

I take another order and go back to the bar, waiting until Slim makes his way toward me.

"A Jack and Coke and two Millers."

He doesn't say anything as he fills the order, but it's busy as hell tonight and we're both running on steam. My feet ache, and my shorts are a bit too small, but then again it's what gets me those killer tips.

I might dress so I show off a bit of skin, but I'm not easy. And if any of these assholes knew I was a virgin, that I've never even been felt up because I chose that, because I wanted it as a consenting adult, they would probably become even more disgusting than they already are.

I turn and look at the bar, the crowd thick, the air hot and heavy. This place is such a dump, with half the customers missing teeth, their guts hanging over their too-big belt buckles, and the stains on their shirts as prominent as the watermarks that line the ceiling.

I'm about to turn around and grab the orders that Slim put on my tray when I notice the front door swing open. Despite how hot I am, the beads of sweat between my breasts trickling down, I freeze. Chills race along my spine, move over my arms, and I swear it's as if this icy touch has a hold on me.

There, walking in like he owns the damn place—which holy hell, does he ever—is Ryker Stone.

His pants have that worn appearance, and God, does he look good in them. The silver chain that hangs from his pocket and down across his thigh catches the light briefly. He's wearing a t-shirt, that, although it fits him perfectly, also tells of the power he wields.

He's not a huge guy, not muscular like a bodybuilder. But he is tall, toned, ripped in every aspect of the word. He's lean with cuts of muscle that tell a person he'll kick their ass and not have any trouble doing it.

My throat is so dry, my tongue suddenly feeling too thick. He's older than me, by a couple decades, in fact. But I don't care about any of that.

I have wanted him since I was sixteen years old and saw him working under the hood of a car. Grease had covered him in the best of ways. And his hands—God, his hands—are so big, with veins that are roped up his muscular forearms. Every time I see them my legs get weak, I grow wet between my legs, and my breathing becomes ragged as I think of all the things he could do to me with those hands. I might be a virgin, but it's purely by choice. I'm not shy about the things I want… It's just I want those things with Ryker Stone. He makes me think filthy thoughts.

I look into his face and take in his beard, one I image pressed between my thighs as he eats me out…

"Order up," Slim shouts over the music so I can hear.

I force myself to turn around, grab the tray, and deliver the drinks. But even though I'm not looking at Ryker I can feel his gaze on me. I swear it's like he's taking my clothes off, just tearing the material from my body so he can get to the good parts.

And God, do I want him to get to the good parts.

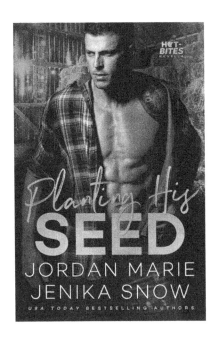

Carson

"When's Virginia's plane due in?" Mavis asks.

I don't turn around to look at her. I'm standing at the large picture window in my study, looking out across the land that has been in my family for generations. Land that has seeped into my bones and oozes out when I bleed. Land that is a part of me. Land I would die without.

Living in Blayton, Wyoming might not be for everyone, but it's all I've ever known—and all I've ever wanted. *Except for one thing.*

Virginia Madison.

I've wanted Jenny for as long as I can remember. She's been my biggest blessing and my biggest curse. Her father, Luke, was older than me, but he was my best friend and someone I trusted and leaned on. Being a farmer in the heart of ranch country isn't fucking easy. Being a farmer anywhere these days is hell. Luke

EXCERPT: PLANTING HIS SEED

was a sounding board when I needed it. I depended on him every damn day and I think he did the same with me.

When cancer took him out six years ago it felt like I lost a piece of myself. I had already lost both of my parents and except for Luke and this land I didn't really have anyone. I'd do anything for Luke, and when he asked me to take care of his daughter, I agreed—against my better judgment. What the hell does a thirty-year-old hardened bachelor know about sixteen-year-old girls—other than they're trouble?

And Jenny is definitely that.

She was angry at the world after losing her father. She had no one left either and if anyone knew that feeling, it was me. We settled into a routine. I was never her father, would never try to be. I became her guardian and her friend and that was fine. My housekeeper Mavis was more of a parental role for Jenny.

For the first year, it worked out great. I began to look forward to spending time in the evenings listening to Jenny talk about school and her plans for the future. Hell, I didn't even mind listening to hours and hours of talk about her friends. Slowly that changed. At seventeen, Jenny began dating. Fuck, I might have been thirty-one at the time, but I still remembered what seventeen-year-old boys did and what stayed on their minds. I had to watch Jenny like a hawk. I owed it to Luke to make sure no one took advantage of his little girl. That's all it was.

Until it wasn't.

One night, on the eve of her eighteenth birthday, we were on the front porch watching the stars, reminiscing about her father and the past and that's when it happened.

We kissed.

It wasn't planned or premeditated. It happened from bonding over common grief. I had no business touching her. I'm fourteen years older than her, she was placed in my care by her father, and I am supposed to look out for her. Hell, I'm supposed to protect her from perverts trying to get in her pants—not become one of them.

I've fought it. I've fought it for four years. I found excuses to stay away from her until I could get my libido under control. Then, I made sure she went all the way to Florida for college. That almost killed me, because with just one touch of her lips I became a marked man. There was only one woman I wanted, and one woman I had to have from that moment on.

Over the years I've become an expert at keeping my body's reactions hidden from Jenny. Every time she came home for the holidays or during breaks, I was both in heaven and in hell. Having her close to me, hugging her and just spending time with her was an exercise…in torture. Jenny, for her part, was and is clueless. She has no idea how much I want her or how much I *need* her. She has no idea about all of the dirty little things I want to do to her body.

I pull my gaze from the window and the landscape outside, to the well-worn photo in my hand. It's a picture of Jenny from last Christmas. Her long brown hair is pulled back on the top of her head in a ponytail, and stops at her lower back. Her sparkling green eyes shine like they have the answers to life's greatest mysteries. She's tall and slim. She's too slim if I'm being honest.

Some damn boyfriend she had convinced her she was too heavy and she ended up going to the gym religiously. That little asshole didn't last long. I had to work to get rid of him. Jenny deserved better than him. Hell, she deserves better than me. But tonight she's coming home. She's done with school, having earned her bachelor's in education.

In three days she turns twenty-two. I'm done waiting and

EXCERPT: PLANTING HIS SEED

holding back. I've fought with my guilt. I've warred with my conscience, but in the end I don't have a choice. Jenny will be mine.

"She'll be home in a few hours," I tell Mavis. "Make sure everything is ready for her."

"Pfft... Like I wouldn't have the place ready for our girl. Everything is ready, don't you worry. Ole' Mavis is going to make sure everything is perfect for her."

I nod, but I don't answer. I want everything to be perfect. It needs to be. Because I'm claiming her. Jenny doesn't know it yet, but she's my future. She always has been. I was just too blind to see it, to accept it. I'm going to marry her and I'm not even going to let her catch her breath before I claim her body, plant my seed deep inside of her and make sure it takes root. I'll tie her to me in the most elemental way a man can. She'll give me a son to guide this land into the next generation and a beautiful daughter with her mother's glowing green eyes for me to protect. Jenny will give me everything.

I won't stop until she does...

Made in the USA
Middletown, DE
21 August 2022

71912865R00050